No Peas for Nellie

Story and pictures by Chris L. Demarest

Aladdin Books
Macmillan Publishing Company   New York
Collier Macmillan Canada   Toronto
Maxwell Macmillan International Publishing Group
New York   Oxford   Singapore   Sydney

For Joey

First Aladdin Books edition 1991. Copyright © 1988 by Chris L. Demarest. All rights reserved. No part of this book may be reproduced or transmitted in any form or by any means, electronic or mechanical, including photocopying, recording, or by any information storage and retrieval system, without permission in writing from the Publisher. Aladdin Books, Macmillan Publishing Company, 866 Third Avenue, New York, N.Y. 10022. Collier Macmillan Canada, Inc., 1200 Eglinton Avenue East, Suite 200, Don Mills, Ontario M3C 3N1. Printed in the United States of America.
1 2 3 4 5 6 7 8 9 10.
A hardcover edition of *No Peas for Nellie* is available from Macmillan Publishing Company.
Library of Congress Cataloging-in-Publication Data Demarest, Chris L. No peas for Nellie/Chris L. Demarest. – 1st Aladdin Books ed.
p.   cm. Summary: Nellie tells her parents all the things she would rather eat than her peas (spider, aardvarks, crocodile), and while doing so she finishes them all. ISBN 0-689-71474-2 [1. Peas – Fiction.] I. Title. [PZ7.D3914No 1991] [E] – dc20   90–39986   CIP   AC

No Peas for Nellie

Nellie doesn't like peas.

"Peas are good for you," her mother said at dinner.
"Try them one at a time."
"No. No peas," said Nellie. "I don't like them."

"No peas, no dessert," said her father.
"Well, then, maybe just one," said Nellie.
"But there are other things I'd rather eat.

I'd rather eat

a big, furry spider

or a wet, slimy salamander.

I'd have a big helping

of hairy warthog,

followed by
a pair of aardvarks

and a python.

Now, that would be good. YUM!

I'd even rather eat

a big, old crocodile

or a water buffalo—

with salt and pepper, of course.

And watch out, Mr. Lion.
I'm not through yet. ROAR!

No pea could be as tasty
as a serving of giraffe.

And then an elephant, trunk and all—

Yes, that would be perfect. DELICIOUS!"

Nellie sat back and smiled.

"Those are the things I'd rather eat."

"Thank you, Nellie, for eating all your peas,"
said her mother.

"Now would you please finish your milk?"
said her father.

"You know what?" said Nellie.

"There are other things I'd rather drink."